Meet M and M.

Mandy and Mimi were friends.

They were such good friends that sometimes they pretended to be twins.

They both had straight brown hair—with tangles on the same side.

They both had the same front tooth missing.

And both their names began with M.

That was enough for them!

PUFFIN BOOKS ABOUT M&M:

MEET
M & M

by **Pat Ross**
pictures by **Marylin Hafner**

PUFFIN BOOKS

PUFFIN BOOKS

Published by the Penguin Group

Penguin Putnam Inc., 375 Hudson Street, New York, New York 10014, U.S.A.

Penguin Books Ltd, 27 Wrights Lane, London W8 5TZ, England

Penguin Books Australia Ltd, Ringwood, Victoria, Australia

Penguin Books Canada Ltd, 10 Alcorn Avenue, Toronto, Ontario, Canada M4V 3B2

Penguin Books (N.Z.) Ltd, 182–190 Wairau Road, Auckland 10, New Zealand

Penguin Books Ltd, Registered Offices: Harmondsworth, Middlesex, England

First published in the United States of America by Pantheon Books,
a division of Random House, Inc., 1980
Published in Puffin Books, 1988
Reissued 1997

15 17 19 20 18 16

THE LIBRARY OF CONGRESS HAS CATALOGED THE PREVIOUS PUFFIN BOOKS EDITION
UNDER CATALOG CARD NUMBER: 88-42868.
This edition ISBN 0-14-038731-5

Printed in the United States of America

RL: 2.6

For Erica
and for her friend Melissa
P.R.

For my dear friend, Hannah
M.H.

MEET
M & M

ONE

Mandy and Mimi were friends.
They were such good friends
that sometimes they pretended
to be twins.
But Mandy was two inches taller.
So she bent her legs
to look shorter.
And Mimi was one size bigger.
So she held in her stomach
to look smaller.
Then she stood on her toes
to look taller.
But . . .

They both had straight brown hair—
with tangles on the same side
where they chewed it.
They both had the same
front tooth missing.
And both their names began with M.
That was enough for them!
Every day after school,
Mandy climbed the back stairs
of the apartment building

where they both lived.
She always took two steps at a time
from her apartment 2B
to Mimi's apartment 3B.
Or Mimi hopped down the stairs
backwards for twenty hops
without stopping.

"We are the twins, M and M,"
they told everyone they met.
"We stick together like glue!"
They grew out their bangs
and looked shaggy together.
They shared fancy hair clips—
Mandy's red ones with the stars,
and Mimi's silver ones
that sparkled in the dark.

"Rub-a-dub-dub,

M and M in the tub,"

they sang at bath time.

They took turns piling bubbles

in the yellow pail

that belonged to *both* of them.

10

Mandy let Mimi use
her mother's new electric toothbrush.
So Mimi let Mandy try on
her mother's new velvet coat
with the tags still on.
Mandy shared Baby,
her guinea pig.
Mimi shared Maxi,
her dog.

YOUR PRICES ARE OUTRAGEOUS!

They invented the
Haunted House Game and made
scary spiders to tape on the walls.
They played store with
cans of food from the kitchen.
The shopper always complained
about the prices.

The clerk always said,
"We do our best, lady."

They had great times
playing tricks.
They hid Maxi's doggie treats
in the umbrella stand.
Once they hid Baby
in someone's shoe.
And no one ever knew which one
had played the trick.
Sometimes people forgot
who was Mandy and who was Mimi.
Those two were always together.
"Just call us M and M,"
they would say.

TWO

One crabby day everything went wrong.
Mandy and Mimi argued
about what games to play
and how to play them.
Finally, they decided
playing cards would be fun.

But then, they argued
over *where* to play!
After that,
Mandy would not let Mimi
pet Baby on her special pillow—
not even once.
That same day, Mimi showed Mandy
her new box of markers
in twenty exciting colors.
But she only let Mandy *look*.

Before they knew it,

they had one awful fight.

"You Dummy!" screamed Mimi.

"You Big Jerk!" screamed Mandy.

Maxi barked at both of them.

And that was that.

Mimi went home to 3B.

She said she was never

ever coming back.

Mandy called out,

"Who cares?"

And she slammed the door so hard

she hit her elbow on the wall.

They knew each other's
phone number by heart.
And most of the time
when they got mad
they called back in a few minutes
and said, "Want to play?"
That always meant, "I'm sorry."
But this time the phone did not ring.

That very day Mandy hid in the curtains
and watched Mimi walk Maxi.
Later on, Mimi watched Mandy
ride her bike with Tommy from 3C.

The next day,
they met in the elevator going down.
The first thing Mimi said was,
"I'm going to the circus with Tommy."
"Well, I've already been—two times,"
said Mandy.
When the elevator got to the lobby,
they didn't even say goodbye.

That same afternoon,

Mandy sold lemonade

on one side of the big front doors.

And Mimi sold lemonade

on the other side.

Mandy's sign said:

THE BEST IN THIS CITY!

Mimi's sign said:

MUCH BETTER!

Mandy sold one cup
for five cents.
So Mimi sold one cup
plus an extra sip
for five cents.

So Mandy sold one cup
plus an extra sip
plus a free straw
for five cents.

So Mimi sold one cup

plus an extra sip

plus a free straw

plus a song

for five cents.

Mandy thought that was dumb.

And she said so.

Then she took her lemonade stand

back inside.

That night at Mimi's house
the phone rang three times.
Mimi ran to get it first.
But all three calls were
for the babysitter,
who talked to her friends all night.

That night at Mandy's house
the phone rang twice.
Mandy ran to get it first.
But not one call was for her.

THREE

On the third day, the rain came down
like a cold shower.
Mimi sat alone in her room
with Maxi in 3B.
Maxi was glad to have Mimi there.
He rubbed his sloppy mouth
all over Mimi's face
giving her kisses.

But Mimi was not in the mood

for dog kisses.

She was in the mood

for the biggest bubble bath ever.

But before long,

most of the good bubbles had gone away.

Only gray water was left,

and a dirty ring.

It was just no fun

taking a bubble bath alone.

Downstairs in 2B, Mandy tried to play
the Haunted House Game alone.
But the game was not scary at all.
So she decided to play with Baby.
But Baby just slept.
Mandy got out her old, dry markers
and wet them.
But the colors were not
bright and pretty on the paper.

Tap, tap, tap.

Mandy heard a noise.

She thought it must be the rain.

But the rain had stopped.

Tap, tap, tap . . .

Mandy looked out the window.

There, hanging from a rope,

was a yellow pail.

It was *their* yellow bathtub pail!
Mandy opened the window
and pulled the pail
over the window guard

and into her room.
There was something inside—
a flat square package
wrapped in silver foil.

Carefully, she opened the little square.

Inside was a bright picture of Maxi.

And a note that said:

TO M— DO YOU WANT A MARKER?
WHAT COLOR?
—FROM
M.

Quickly, Mandy wet her black marker,
the only one that worked.
And she wrote back:

TO M — How about PurPLe?
              From M.

She wrapped the note in the silver foil
and put it back in the pail.

Then she put Baby's special pillow
in the pail, too.
The rope was still tight.
She gave it a little pull.
Then out the window went the pail,
and up to 3B.

A few minutes later,
down came the pail with the pillow
and a short note that said:
MAXI TRIED TO CHEW IT UP!

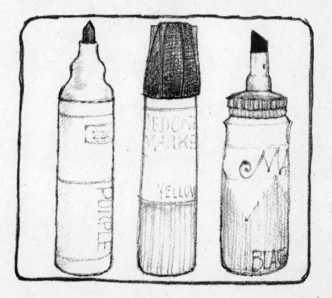

In the pail, Mandy also found
three markers—
the purple one, a yellow one,
and a black that worked.

All afternoon, Mandy and Mimi
sent the pail back and forth.
They sent
small pictures,
racing cars,
one hairbrush,
crackers in a plastic bag,
comic books,
a puzzle with only two pieces missing,
and a million notes.

The last note from Mandy said:

Meet me on the stairs.

Mimi sent one back that said:

JUST WHAT I WAS THINKING!

Mimi raced down the back stairs,
hopping fast.
Mandy raced up the back stairs,
two at a time.

They met halfway,
where they sat and talked
about what to do
tomorrow.

Pat Ross, a former children's book editor and a founder of Feminists on Children's Media, is the author of numerous books for children and adults. She was inspired to write *Meet M&M* by her daughter Erica, who lived in an apartment house just like M and M's. Ms. Ross lives in New York City.

Marylin Hafner has worked as an art director and a magazine illustrator, in addition to illustrating more than two dozen books for young readers. She lives in Cambridge, Massachusetts.